Darby Creek Elementary School

D1441241

EARTH DAY

HOLIDAY CELEBRATIONS

Jason Cooper

Rourke

Publishing LLC

Vero Beach, Florida 32964

www.rourkepublishing.com

PHOTO CREDITS: Cover, p. 4, 8, 13, 17, 21 © Lynn M. Stone; title page courtesy NASA; p. 7, 14 courtesy Earth Day New York; p. 10, 12 courtesy Earth Day Canada; p. 18 © Fritz Albert, courtesy The Wilderness Society.

Cover: *Children gather by a pond to see water creatures and clean up shore litter.*

Editor: Frank Sloan

Cover design by Nicola Stratford

Library of Congress Cataloging-in-Publication Data

Cooper, Jason, 1942-
   Earth Day / Jason Cooper
      p. cm. — (Holiday celebrations)
Includes bibliographical references and index.
Contents: Earth Day — April 22 — Earth Day awareness — Helping the environment — Caring for the environment — Earth Day 1970 — After Earth Day — Laws to improve the environment — Protecting plants and animals.
 ISBN 1-58952-218-4
1. Earth day—Juvenile literature. 2. Environmental protection—Juvenile literature. [1. Earth Day. 2. Environmental protection. 3. Holidays.] I. Title. II. Holiday celebrations (Vero Beach, Fla.)
GE195.5 .C66 2002
333.72—dc21   2002002387

Printed in the USA

PC/CG

TABLE OF CONTENTS

Earth Day   5

April 22   6

Earth Day Awareness   9

Helping the Environment   11

Caring for the Environment   14

Earth Day, 1970   16

After Earth Day   19

Laws to Improve the Environment   20

Protecting Plants and Animals   22

Glossary   23

Index   24

Further Reading/Websites to Visit   24

EARTH DAY

Earth Day is a day for people to pay extra attention to the **environment**. Land, air, and water make up our natural environment. On Earth Day, people work to do good things for the environment.

Earth Day is a working day, but it is also a day of **celebration**. People celebrate the beauty of the environment. They celebrate **progress** in the care of the environment. They learn more about the environment and how to take care of it.

On Earth Day people of all ages learn more about their environment and how to care for it.

5

APRIL 22

Earth Day is held on April 22 of each year in Canada and the United States. The first Earth Day was celebrated in the United States in 1970. It has grown, however. More than 150 nations celebrate Earth Day. In Canada, nearly every school takes part in an Earth Day activity. In some parts of Canada, Earth Day has even grown to become Earth Week!

Celebrating Earth Day in New York City with a parade

EARTH DAY AWARENESS

Earth Day has always been popular with **activists**. Activists are people who get involved. They see a problem and work to help fix that problem. Earth Day activists help make other people aware of the environment's problems. One huge **environmental** problem, for example, is **pollution**.

HELPING THE ENVIRONMENT

Millions of people have found interesting and useful ways to help the environment on Earth Day. Gathering trash from roadsides, beaches, and woodlands is an example of one helpful activity. Planting trees has also been a popular Earth Day activity.

Many Earth Day programs include outdoor fairs and festivals with displays that are both fun and **educational**. Education has always been an important part of Earth Day. After all, people cannot help fix environmental problems until they learn about those problems.

Children in Toronto, Ontario, Canada, plant trees on Earth Day.

Children and adults spread out across Downsview Park near Toronto to plant trees on Earth Day.

Earth Day lessons about caring for the environment can last throughout the year and a lifetime.

CARING FOR THE ENVIRONMENT

In the 1960s, America showed little care for its environment. Wisconsin Governor Gaylord Nelson was among those most concerned. He wanted to find a way to make people understand the serious environmental problems around them. He especially wanted government groups to act in the environment's favor.

Children and adults dressed as frogs enjoy an Earth Day parade in New York City.

EARTH DAY, 1970

In 1969, when Gaylord Nelson was a U.S. senator, he had an idea. College students across the country were rising up against the war in Vietnam. But students, Senator Nelson knew, cared about the environment as well as the war. Senator Nelson decided to call for public **demonstrations** in support of the environment.

The idea took off. College students turned out, but so did many adults. Some 20 million Americans showed up at Earth Day activities on April 22, 1970.

Serious environmental problems in 1970 included the clear cutting of huge areas of forest.

AFTER EARTH DAY

The North American environment still needs all the help it can find. But Earth Day worked as Senator Nelson hoped it would. It caught the attention of the **politicians**. Politicians are the mayors, governors, senators, presidents and others who work in government.

Former U.S. Senator Gaylord Nelson was a founder of Earth Day in 1970.

LAWS TO IMPROVE
THE ENVIRONMENT

In the months and years after Earth Day, 1970, the United States Government passed several laws to improve the environment. New rules were passed to force **polluters** to clean up their factories, ships, and cars. Air and water quality were improved. The use of DDT was stopped. DDT was a poison used to kill insects, but it was also killing millions of birds, including bald eagles.

The bald eagle returned to American skies after the use of DDT ended.

PROTECTING PLANTS AND ANIMALS

A law called the Endangered Species Act passed. It gave protection to hundreds of kinds of plants and animals that had become rare.

No question about it: Earth Day has made the environment better for everyone.

GLOSSARY

activists (ACK tuh vists) — those who actively support a cause or idea

celebration (SELL uh BRAY shun) — public display of joyfulness

demonstrations (DEM un STRAY shuns) — public gatherings in order to protest

educational (ED you kay shun ul) — that which helps people learn

environment (en VYE run ment) — air, land, water, and other things that make up our surroundings

environmental (en VYE run men tul) — having to do with the environment, our surroundings

politicians (pol uh TISH unz) — people elected to public office to help consider ideas, laws, and practices

polluter (puh LOOT ur) — a person or company that is guilty of putting harmful material into the environment

pollution (puh LOO shun) — harmful material in the environment

progress (PROG russ) — steps made to help something

INDEX

activists   9

Canada   6

DDT   20

eagles, bald   20

Earth Day   5, 6, 9, 11, 19

education   11

Endangered Species Act   22

environment   5, 11, 14, 16, 19, 20

Nelson, Gaylord   14, 16

politicians   19

pollution   9

United States   6

U.S. Government   20

Further Reading

Ansary, Mir Tamim. *Earth Day*. Heinemann Library, 2001.

Roop, Connie. *Let's Celebrate Earth Day*. Millbrook Press, 2001.

Websites To Visit

Earth Day Canada at http://www.earthday.ca

Earth Day on line at http://earthday.envirolink.org/history.html

About The Author

Jason Cooper has written several children's books about a variety of topics for Rourke Publishing, including recent series *China Discovery* and *American Landmarks*. Cooper travels widely to gather information for his books. Two of his favorite travel destinations are Alaska and the Far East.